Courtney Crumrin

By Ted Naifeh

Monstrous Holiday

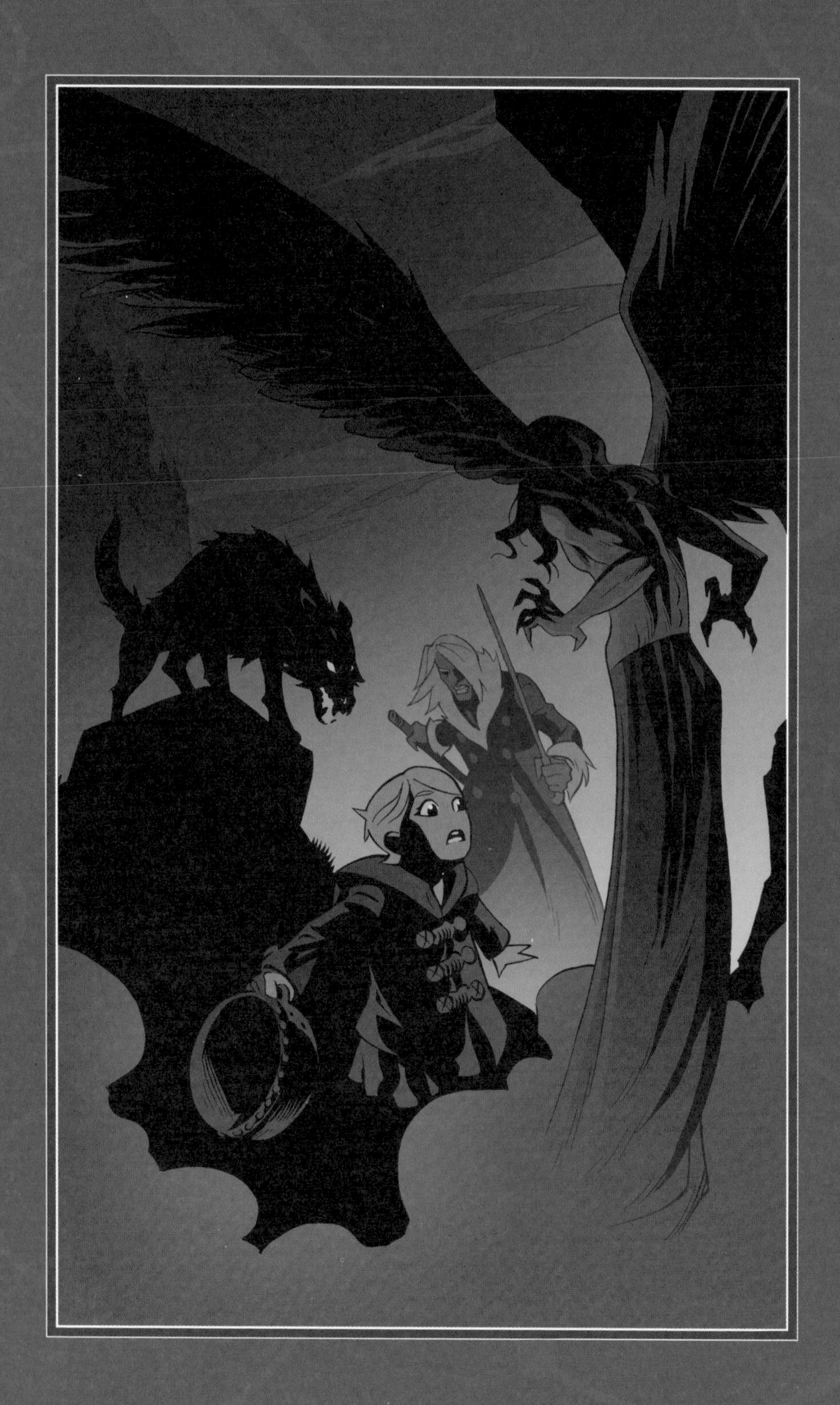

Courtney Crumrin

By Ted Naifeh

Monstrous Holiday

Written & Illustrated by
Ted Naifeh

Colored by
Warren Wucinich

Original Series edited by
Joe Nozemack, James Lucas Jones, and Jill Beaton

Collection edited by
Robin Herrera

Design by
Keith Wood and Angie Knowles

Originally published as *The Fire Thief's Tale* and *The Prince of Nowhere*.

1319 SE Martin Luther King Jr. Blvd.
Suite 240
Portland, OR 97214

onipress.com · tednaifeh.com
facebook.com/onipress · twitter.com/onipress
onipress.tumblr.com · instagram.com/onipress

First Edition: January 2019

ISBN 978-1-62010-569-6
eISBN 978-1-62010-035-6

1 3 5 7 9 10 8 6 4 2

Library of Congress Control Number: 2013938917

Printed in China.

For Kelly

Chapter One

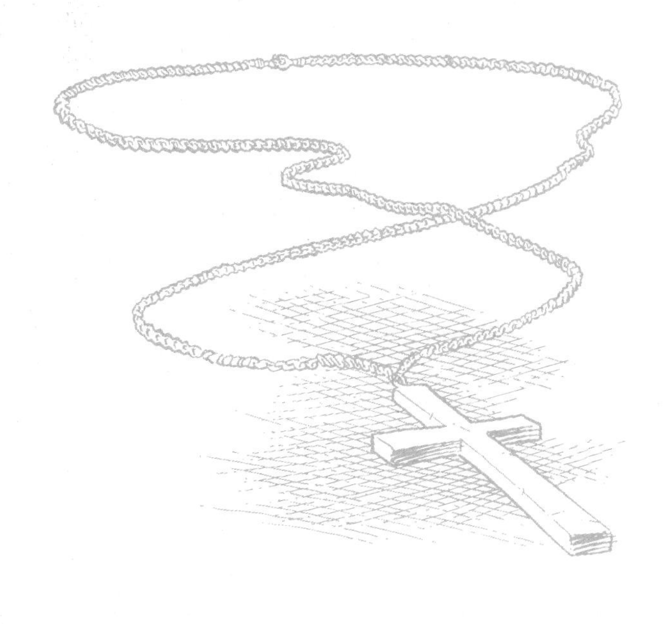

ARRRRROOOOOOOOOO

THERE YOU ARE.

WON'T THAT CURSED HOWLING EVER-

-STOP...
BANG

KRASH

DON'T WORRY, MY DEAR.

ALOYSIUS! THIS IS AN UNEXPECTED SURPRISE.

IT WOULDN'T BE SO UNEXPECTED IF YOU'D JUST GET YOURSELF A TELEPHONE.
AND WHO'S YOUR COMPANION?
THIS IS MY GRAND-NIECE, COURTNEY.

COURTNEY, THIS IS PROFESSOR ALEXI MARKOVIC, ONE OF MY OLDEST FRIENDS.
DON'T BE SHY, MY DEAR.

I'M GLAD YOU'RE **HERE**. I'VE MANAGED TO UNEARTH THIS OLD **TEXT**, AND I'D LOVE TO HEAR WHAT YOU **THINK** OF IT.
INDEED? WHAT **IS** IT?
OH, IT'S **QUITE** REMARKABLE.

HAVE YOU EVER HEARD ANY TRUE ACCOUNTS OF **LYCANTHROPY?**
ONCE OR TWICE. GO **ON**.

DON'T **BOTHER**.

IT'S SEALED BY POWERS YOU CAN'T EVEN **FATHOM**.
THAT **SO?**

THERE YOU ARE, MY DARLING.
PETRU!

DID YOU...
NO LUCK TONIGHT, ALAS.

OUR QUARRY ESCAPED.

BUT WE'LL GET IT, YOU'LL SEE.

IT'S RIDICULOUS, YOU OUT THERE HUNTING WOLVES LIKE A BUNCH OF EIGHTEENTH-CENTURY FARMERS. YOU SHOULD JUST CALL ANIMAL CONTROL.

AH, THERE YOU ARE. NO LUCK, EH?
YOU KNOW VERY WELL WHY WE CAN'T DO THAT, BELOVED.

YOU REMEMBER MY OLD FRIEND PROFESSOR CRUMRIN.
ALOYSIUS, PETRU HERE IS NOW BETROTHED TO MY DAUGHTER. THEY'RE TO BE WED NEXT WEEK.
CONGRATULATIONS, YOUR GRACE.

NOW NOW, MR. CRUMRIN. WE'VE DISCUSSED THIS BEFORE.
MY FAMILY RENOUNCED THE DUCAL TITLE ALMOST A CENTURY AGO.
THAT WAS HUMBLE OF THEM. THOUGH I GATHER THEY HUNG ONTO THE WEALTH.
AND IT'S "PROFESSOR CRUMRIN."
FATHER-
MAGDA WAS STILL A CHILD WHEN YOU LAST SAW HER, WASN'T SHE?

SHE'S GROWN INTO SUCH A PRETTY YOUNG WOMAN, HASN'T SHE?
FASCINATING.
DARLING, WHY DON'T YOU FETCH SOME SLIVOVITZ FOR THE MEN.

HELLO, MAGDA.

HMPH!

COURTNEY HAD BEEN TRAVELING WITH HER UNCLE FOR ALMOST A WEEK. THEY DIDN'T TALK MUCH.

STILL, IT WAS THE HAPPIEST TIME COURTNEY COULD REMEMBER.
YEAH YEAH, QUIT FUSSING.
YOU KNOW, FOR A GIRL WHO'S ABOUT TO GET MARRIED, THAT MAGGY ISN'T EXACTLY GLOWING.
WE ALL SHOW JOY IN OUR OWN WAY.

WHAT'S THIS?
JUST SOME BED-TIME READING I PICKED UP.

BUT I THINK I'M TOO TIRED.
STILL JETLAGGED, EH? I SUPPOSE YOU'RE TOO OLD FOR A BEDTIME STORY.

I'VE NEVER HAD ONE. UNLESS YOU COUNT MOM TELLING ME ABOUT HER AFTER-CHRISTMAS SHOPPING TRIUMPHS.

ONCE UPON A TIME, THERE WERE TWO BROTHERS WHO LIVED IN THE FOREST.

IT WAS A TIME BEFORE CITIES AND CIVILIZATION, WHEN MEN WERE JUST ANOTHER ANIMAL IN THE FOREST, ALBEIT AN UNUSUALLY **CLEVER** ONE.
BUT THESE BROTHERS **WEREN'T** MEN. THEY WERE **WOLVES**.

IT WAS A **DIRE** WINTER. THERE WAS LITTLE TO **EAT** AND NO SHELTER FROM THE **COLD**.
THE BROTHERS WERE **DYING**.

ONE NIGHT, THEY CAME UPON SOMETHING **CURIOUS**.

"THIS CREATURE HAS FOUND A LITTLE PIECE OF THE **SUN**," SAID THE YOUNGER BROTHER. "LET US **SLAY** HIM, AND THE WARMTH WILL BE **OURS**."

"**NO!**" SAID THE ELDER BROTHER. "THAT IS A **MAN**. HE HAS A LONG **TOOTH** THAT FLIES THROUGH THE **AIR**. OUR FATHER WAS **SLAIN** BY SUCH A BEAST, **REMEMBER**?"

LONG THEY WATCHED. AT LAST, THE YOUNGER BROTHER SAID, "IF WE DON'T DO SOMETHING, WE SHALL DIE."

PERHAPS THE OLDER WOLF'S MIND SNAPPED. PERHAPS THE COLD AND HUNGER HAD BROKEN HIS SPIRIT.

"PLEASE," HE BEGGED HIS ENEMY. "PLEASE, MAY I SHARE YOUR FIRE?"

SIT!

GOOD BOY. DOWN!

AND SO, HE BECAME THE FIRST DOG.

THE YOUNGER WOLF WATCHED BITTERLY...

...WATCHED AS HIS ELDER BROTHER, LEADER OF PACKS AND MIGHTY HUNTER, ATE THE LEAVINGS OF ANOTHER CREATURE'S MEAL.

BUT THE COLD PIERCED HIS HEART, AND THE WARMTH OF THE FIRE BECKONED.
SIT!

AND IN THAT MOMENT, THE YOUNG WOLF KNEW WHAT HE MUST DO.
I SAID SIT!!!

THE FIRE BURNED HIS FACE. BUT HIS TEETH CLOSED ON WHAT HE WANTED.

HE RAN AS FAST AS ANY WOLF COULD RUN.
HIS BROTHER KNEW IT WOULDN'T BE FAST ENOUGH.

AARGH!

ALL THAT FOLLOWED HIM WERE THE CRIES AND WHIMPERS OF HIS BROTHER AS THE MAN BEAT HIM.

AND THUS, HE BECAME THE FIRST...

GOODNIGHT, LITTLE ONE.

COURTNEY'S JET LAG NOT ONLY MADE HER SLUGGISH ALL AFTERNOON...

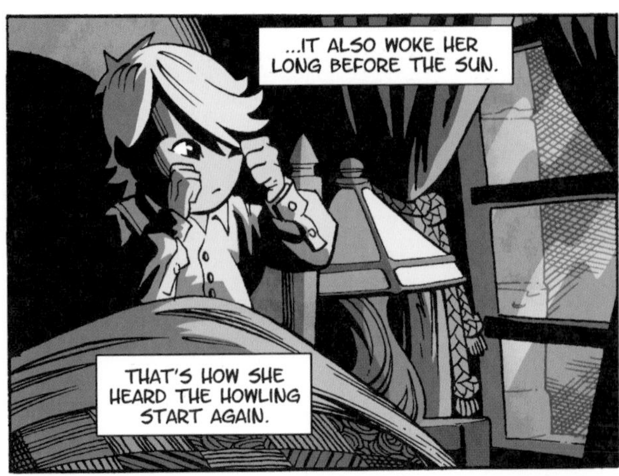
...IT ALSO WOKE HER LONG BEFORE THE SUN.
THAT'S HOW SHE HEARD THE HOWLING START AGAIN.

AND THAT'S HOW SHE ALSO SAW...
HUH...

IF YOU'VE OBSERVED COURTNEY FOR AS LONG AS I HAVE, YOU ALREADY KNOW WHAT A CURIOUS GIRL SHE IS.

IN MY HUMBLE OPINION, THE WORD "BUSYBODY" WOULDN'T BE TOO STRONG.

AND THIS ISN'T THE FIRST TIME IT'S GOTTEN HER INTO TROUBLE.

STUPID! STUPID! STUPID!
Rrrraaawwwlll!

Slam
>PHEW<

AND THEN I PEEKED OUT THE WINDOW...

AND THERE WAS NOTHING THERE.
WHADAYA THINK? WEIRD, HUH?
FRANKLY, COURTNEY, I'M NOT IMPRESSED.

WHAT ON EARTH POSSESSED YOU TO VENTURE OUT ALONE, WHEN YOU KNEW A WOLF WAS PROWLING THE FOREST?
I... I THOUGHT...
DID YOU? SHOCKING.

LISTEN TO ME, YOUNG LADY. SO FAR YOU SEEM BLESSED WITH STUPIDITY AND LUCK IN EQUAL MEASURE.
HOWEVER, LUCK ALWAYS RUNS OUT, WHEREAS YOUR WELLSPRING OF STUPIDITY SEEMS BOUNDLESS.

AND I WON'T ALWAYS BE THERE.

BEFORE COURTNEY COULD EVEN FORMULATE A REPLY...

...THE THREAD OF HER THOUGHTS WAS YANKED AWAY.

AHEM.

YOU'RE TOO KIND.

SEE TO IT I STAY THAT WAY.

SHE'D SEEN PLACES THAT SIMPLY TOOK HER BREATH AWAY.

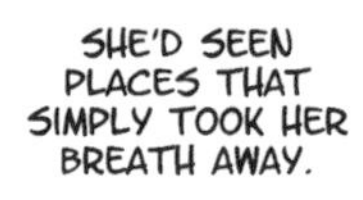

THEY WON'T TRY ANYTHING IN PUBLIC AGAIN.
PLEASE JAN, GO AWAY. IF THEY SAW YOU WITH ME-

DON'T BE SO SURE. YOU CAN'T EXPECT THE POLICE TO APPEAR EVERY TIME.
IT DOESN'T MATTER. I NEED TO TELL YOU...

WE'RE LEAVING. WE'VE BEEN HERE TOO LONG AS IT IS. DRAGOMIR IS ANXIOUS ABOUT ME.
OH.
IF YOU CAME AWAY WITH US...

AND WHAT CAN YOU OFFER ME AS A HUSBAND? LONELY HOURS WAITING TO HEAR IF YOU'VE SURVIVED THE NIGHT?

OR IF YOU'VE DONE SOMETHING DREADFUL? YOU SHOULD HAVE TOLD ME WHAT YOU WERE, JAN.
MORNING, GYPSY BOY.

SORRY I MISSED YOU LAST NIGHT. IT WON'T HAPPEN AGAIN.

YOU'D BETTER HOPE NOT. YOU WON'T GET A THIRD CHANCE.

STOP IT, BOTH OF YOU. YOU'RE ACTING LIKE CHILDREN.
I DON'T THINK WE SHOULD WAIT FOR NIGHTFALL, DO YOU BOYS?

AFTER ALL, WE'RE COMMUNITY LEADERS. WE SHOULD SET AN EXAMPLE.

IF THAT'S THE CASE, CAN YOU GUYS SHOW ME WHERE THE CATHEDRAL IS? I NEED TO CONFESS MY SINS.

UMM...
LISTEN PETRU, MAYBE WE SHOULDN'T...
I KNOW YOU, DON'T I?

YES, OF COURSE. THE AMERICAN SORCERER'S GRANDCHILD.
NIECE.
TRYING TO INTERFERE, EH? I KNOW OLD CRUMRIN IS FRIENDLY WITH THESE DEVILS.

LISTEN, YOU BETTER JUST BACK OFF.
OR YOU'LL HEX ME, EH?

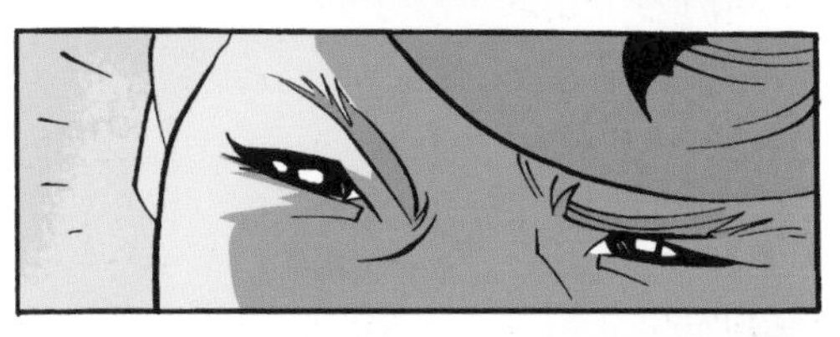

YOU SEE, GENTLEMEN, HOW THE LITTLE WITCH USED THE EVIL EYE?

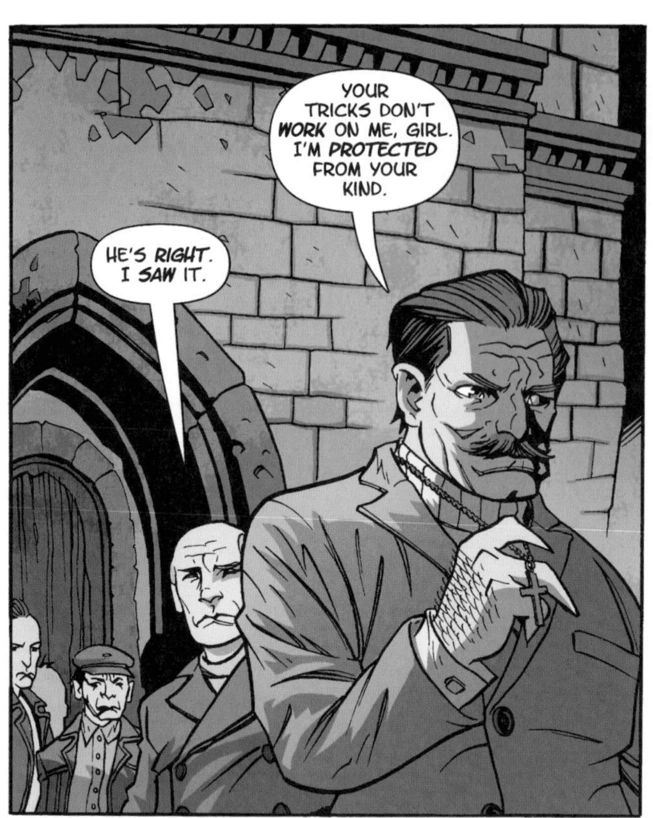
YOUR TRICKS DON'T WORK ON ME, GIRL. I'M PROTECTED FROM YOUR KIND.
HE'S RIGHT. I SAW IT.

I'LL SHOW YOU WHAT WE DO TO WITCHES IN THIS TOWN.

ARE YOU GENTLEMEN HAVING TROUBLE WITH MY NIECE?

BECAUSE I CAN ASSURE YOU, IF THERE'S ONE THING I CAN HELP WITH, IT'S TROUBLE.

I'M SURE YOU RECOGNIZE THIS *TALISMAN*, SORCERER. YOUR *FRIEND*, FATHER *MARKOVIC*, LENT IT TO ME.

I'VE NOTHING TO *FEAR* FROM YOUR KIND.

INDEED?
WHAT ABOUT *POLICEMEN?*

AT IT *AGAIN*, MR. BOGDAN? FOR *GOODNESS'* *SAKE*, CAN'T YOU LEAVE THAT BOY *ALONE?*

DAMN IT, SASHA, I *TOLD* YOU–
HAS *HE* OR HIS *FAMILY* BROKEN ANY *LAWS?* DO YOU WANT TO SUBMIT A *COMPLAINT?*

CAN'T YOU *SEE* WHAT'S GOING *ON* HERE?
ALL TOO *WELL*, SIR.
I THINK THE OFFICER CAN *HANDLE* IT FROM *HERE*.
OW!

YOU'RE HURTING ME!
HAVE YOU GONE DEAF? IS THERE SOMETHING WRONG WITH YOUR MEMORY?

WHAT ARE YOU TALKING ABOUT? THAT GYPSY GUY NEEDS-
YOU NEED TO LISTEN TO ME!

NOT AN HOUR AGO I WARNED YOU ABOUT GETTING INTO DANGEROUS SITUATIONS. THE NEXT MOMENT, I FIND YOU USING WITCHCRAFT ON OUR HOST'S FRIEND.

BUT HE WAS-
ENOUGH!

WHAT'S BETWEEN PETRU, HIS FIANCÉE, AND THAT YOUNG MAN IS NONE OF YOUR BUSINESS OR MINE.

IF I FIND YOU FLINGING YOURSELF INTO DANGER AGAIN...
I'LL SEND YOU HOME.

A SULLEN SILENCE SETTLED BETWEEN COURTNEY AND HER UNCLE. HE HARDLY SEEMED TO NOTICE, WRAPPED UP IN TALK WITH THE OLD PROFESSOR ABOUT DUSTY BOOKS AND MYSTICAL MUMBO-JUMBO.
Knock knock Knock

Knock knock Knock

I ASSURE YOU, SAINT LUCIAN'S POWERS WERE WELL DOCUMENTED. HE BROUGHT SOLDIERS BACK FROM THE BRINK OF DEATH WITH JUST A TOUCH.
OH YES? AND HOW, PRAY, DID HE DO THAT?

Knock knock Knock
WHY, FAITH, SIR, OF COURSE.
ADMIRABLY SIMPLE. THOUGH FOR MY PURPOSES, MORE CONCRETE INSTRUCTIONS WOULD BE PREFERABLE.

Knock Knock Knock
ISN'T ANYONE GOING TO GET THAT?

IS SHE HERE?

LOOK, MAYBE IT'S BETTER IF YOU CAME BACK LATER-
PLEASE, JUST GIVE HER A MESSAGE FOR ME. TELL HER...

TELL HER I'M SORRY. I ONLY WANTED TO BE KIND TO HER.

...

NOW, SEE HERE, YOUNG MAN. I'VE NOTHING AGAINST YOU PERSONALLY.

BUT IF YOU CONTINUE HARASSING MY DAUGHTER, I SHALL CALL THE POLICE.

I'M VERY SORRY, SIR.

COURTNEY TRIED TO SAY SOMETHING, BUT HER THROAT TIGHTENED.

IT WAS HIS EYES THAT GOT HER.
HUGE, BLACK EYES, SO FULL OF LOVE, GRIEF, WARMTH AND HEARTACHE...

MEMORIES CRASHED INTO HER BRAIN LIKE A TIDAL WAVE, ICY WITH THE PAIN OF INCONSOLABLE LOSS.

WAIT! DON'T...

...GO...

GOOD HEAVENS, CHILD! GET BACK IN THE HOUSE!

ALOYSIUS TOOK THE STUNNED COURTNEY TO HER ROOM.

SHE OBEYED MECHANICALLY, AS IF SLEEP-WALKING.
YOU **KNEW**, DIDN'T YOU?
I'VE ENCOUNTERED **OTHERS** OF HIS KIND.

TRY TO GET SOME **SLEEP**. I'LL SEE IF I CAN SCARE UP SOME **EAR PLUGS**.

DON'T WORRY, BOY.

I WON'T MISS YOU AGAIN.

MOTHER OF-

THE HOWLING HADN'T KEPT COURTNEY AWAKE, THOUGH IT LED TO STRANGE, MELANCHOLY DREAMS.

BUT THE TREMENDOUS UPROAR IN THE HALL WOULD HAVE WOKEN THE DEAD.
PROFESSOR! IT'S PETRU!
LORD, PROTECT ME!
PROTECT ME!

WHAT IN HEAVEN'S-
BITTEN! HE WAS BITTEN!

THERE'S A SACRAMENT I FOUND. BUT YOU MUST HAVE FAITH, PETRU.
THERE WERE DOZENS OF THEM!
GET...

GET HIM OUT.

THERE'S NOTHING YOU CAN DO, ALOYSIUS. YOUR SKILLS...
QUITE RIGHT, PROFESSOR.
JUST A THOUGHT, YOU MAY WANT TO CLEAN THAT WOUND ONCE YOU'VE BLESSED IT.

A BUNCH OF FRANTIC PRAYERS WON'T BE MUCH HELP. IF THEY WERE, MY PARENTS WOULD BE BILLIONAIRES BY NOW.

DON'T BE SO CYNICAL, COURTNEY. IF OUR MAGIC WORKS, WHY SHOULDN'T HIS?

HOW DID YOU SUPPOSE YOUR LITTLE JINX FAILED TODAY? THAT CROSS OF PETRU'S IS QUITE A POWERFUL TALISMAN.

IT DIDN'T SAVE HIM, THOUGH, DID IT?

THAT'S MAGIC FOR YOU. WE THINK WE UNDERSTAND IT, BUT WE'RE REALLY JUST MUCKING ABOUT WITH UNKNOWABLE FORCES.

THIS TIME, IT WASN'T JET LAG THAT KEPT COURTNEY AWAKE.

SHE WAS UNSURPRISED TO SEE THAT ALOYSIUS' PROHIBITION FROM DANGER DIDN'T APPLY TO HIMSELF.

HUH...

OH...
SILENTLY, THEY EMERGED. THERE WERE NO SNARLS, NO SNAPPING FANGS. THEY JUST REGARDED HER CURIOUSLY.

AND BEGAN TO GENTLY HERD HER ALONG.
...BUGGER.

THE CAVE MOUTH SPREAD OPEN LIKE AN IRONIC SMILE. YET A WARM LIGHT EMANATED FROM WITHIN.

WHAT SHE FOUND INSIDE WAS THE VERY LAST THING SHE EXPECTED.
AND SO HE BECAME THE FIRST OF US.

I DON'T UNDERSTAND, GRANDFATHER. HOW WOULD A BURNING STICK MAKE A SIMPLE BEAST INTO US?
ARE YOU SAYING WE'RE NOT BEASTS?

DOES THAT MEAN WE'RE HUMAN?
NO, BUT WE'RE NOT LIKE REGULAR WOLVES.
DO YOU WANT TO HEAR THE REST OF THE STORY OR NOT?

THE YOUNGER BROTHER SOON LEARNED TO NURTURE THE FIRE LIKE A CHILD.

IT SEEMED TO IGNITE A FLAME IN HIS HEAD, AND SOON HE HAD MASTERED OTHER HUMAN MAGICS.

IN THE FULLNESS OF TIME, HE MATED AND HAD CHILDREN, SHARING HIS KNOWLEDGE WITH THEM.

AT LAST, IT WAS ALL BUT IMPOSSIBLE TO TELL THE DIFFERENCE BETWEEN WOLF AND MAN.

UNTIL ONE FATEFUL NIGHT...

GOOD EVENING, STRANGER. I'M A LONG WAY FROM MY FIRE, BUT IF YOU'LL SHARE YOURS, I'LL SHARE MY KILL.

THE OLD MAN WAS GRATEFUL, AND TAUGHT THE WOLF HOW TO USE STONE AND TINDER TO LIGHT FIRES ANEW.

ALL WAS CIVIL, UNTIL...

NO! BAD DOG!

IT WAS HIS ELDER BROTHER.

ONCE SATISFIED, THE OLD MAN PASSED THE REMAINS OF HIS MEAL TO THE DOG AND FELL ASLEEP.
HELLO, BROTHER.

I KNEW IT WAS YOU. YOU'VE CHANGED.

I SURVIVED THE PITILESS WINTER. I HAVE FIRE AND FOOD AND FAMILY.

COME! I WILL KILL THE MAN, AND YOU CAN COME BACK WITH ME TO THE FOREST.

I HAVE CHANGED TOO. I BELONG TO HIM NOW, AND HE TO ME.
NO, BROTHER.

HE STARVES YOU AND BEATS YOU.

HE DISCIPLINES ME WHEN MY ANIMAL WAYS TAKE OVER. YET HE CARES FOR ME. I NEVER HAVE MUCH FOOD, BUT ALWAYS GET ENOUGH. HE FOUND ME A MATE, AND CARES FOR OUR PUPS. HE LOVES ME.

AND I SUPPOSE I LOVE HIM.

VERY WELL. BUT HE NEEDS A LESSON...
...SO THAT HE WON'T FORGET WHAT IT'S LIKE...

...TO BE A BEAST.

GRRRRRRRRRRRF
WHA-? NO!

NOOOOO!

AND FROM THAT DAY FORWARD...
...WHEN THE MOON, OUR MOTHER, WAXED FATTEST...
...THE MAN TEMPORARILY LOST HIS MAGIC AND HIS PRETENSIONS.

IT IS OUR CURSE, AND OUR GIFT, FOR MEN WHO FORGET THAT THEY ARE, AFTER ALL, ONLY ANIMALS...
...IF RATHER CLEVER ANIMALS.

WE'RE LEAVING TONIGHT. WE WON'T BE BACK FOR MANY, MANY YEARS.

I'M SORRY FOR WHAT HAPPENED LAST NIGHT. BUT A FATHER MUST PROTECT HIS CHILDREN.

THOUGH I FEAR THIS LITTLE ONE TOOK HIS WORST WOUND ALREADY.

SHE COULD THINK OF NOTHING WORTH SAYING, SO SHE REMAINED SILENT.

YET, AS WITH OTHER ADVENTURES, TO SEE WHAT SHE'D SEEN MADE HER FEEL SOMEHOW BLESSED.

GRRRRRRR

BUT THAT DIDN'T MEAN SHE WANTED TO PRESS HER LUCK.

SHE JUST HOPED SHE COULD GET BACK INTO BED UNNOTICED.

MAGDA!

PLEASE, DON'T LEAVE ME ALONE!

IS ANYONE THERE?

I NEVER WANTED TO MARRY HIM.

FATHER THOUGHT IT WOULD BE A GOOD MATCH. PETRU'S FAMILY IS IMPORTANT. THEY OWN HALF THE VILLAGE.

NOW HE'S TAINTED. HIS WEALTH, HIS NAME, THEY'LL MEAN NOTHING.

WHAT AM I SUPPOSED TO DO? I CAN'T REJECT HIM NOW!
WHY NOT?

WHY NOT DO WHAT YOU WANT TO DO?

YOU'RE JUST A CHILD.

YOU DON'T UNDERSTAND.

NO.
MAGDA? IS THAT YOU?

OH. HAVE YOU COME TO GLOAT, LITTLE WITCH?
I THOUGHT YOU WANTED COMPANY.

I DON'T WANT YOUR PITY.
THAT'S COOL, I WASN'T OFFERING ANY.

YOU THINK I DESERVE TO BECOME AN ANIMAL?

I THINK...
I THINK WHEN YOU HATE SOMETHING HARD ENOUGH, YOU USUALLY END UP LOOKING JUST LIKE IT.

I'VE SEEN IT HAPPEN.

BREAKFAST WAS A SOMBER AFFAIR. PROFESSOR MARKOVIC AND HIS DAUGHTER SPOKE LITTLE AND ATE LESS, EXCUSING THEMSELVES QUICKLY.
JUST WHEN COURTNEY THOUGHT HER ADVENTURE HAD GONE UNNOTICED...
I WONDER IF YOU MIGHT BE WILLING TO EXPLAIN WHY, DESPITE MY WARNINGS, YOU WENT INTO THE FOREST LAST NIGHT.

BUT SHE HAD HER ANSWER READY.
I SAW YOU GO OUT, AND I FIGURED ANYTHING THAT CAUTIOUS, RESPONSIBLE UNCLE A WOULD DO COULDN'T POSSIBLY BE DANGEROUS.

I SEE.

WILL PETRU REALLY TURN INTO A WOLF?

WHO KNOWS? I'VE HEARD STORIES, OBVIOUSLY. WE ALL HAVE.

STORIES?
FOLK TALES OF MEN, ONCE BITTEN, LOSING THEIR MINDS, THEIR SOULS, AND TRANSFORMING INTO MONSTERS.
NOTHING VERIFIABLE, OF COURSE...
DRAGOMIR'S PEOPLE KEEP THEIR SECRETS WELL.

SO, HE'LL BECOME A MONSTER?
FATHER MARKOVIC CAST A PURGING SACRAMENT. IT MIGHT WORK, OR IT MIGHT NOT.

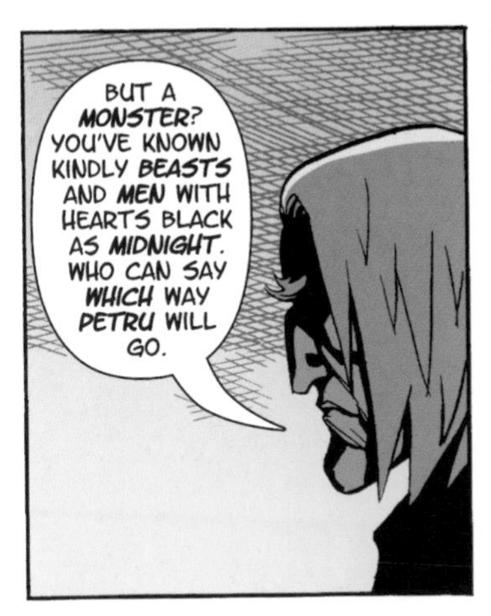
BUT A MONSTER? YOU'VE KNOWN KINDLY BEASTS AND MEN WITH HEARTS BLACK AS MIDNIGHT. WHO CAN SAY WHICH WAY PETRU WILL GO.

HAVE YOU EVER HEARD OF A WEREWOLF AND A... A PERSON... YOU KNOW...
FALLING IN LOVE? AGAIN, ONLY STORIES.

BUT THINK ABOUT IT, COURTNEY. HOW COULD IT END WELL?

THEIR KIND AMONG OURS MUST LIVE A LIFE OF SECRECY, IN CONSTANT DANGER OF DISCOVERY AND DEATH.
BUT WHAT IF...

A HUMAN AMONG THEM WOULD NEVER SURVIVE.

WHY NOT?
THEY MAY BE AS CLEVER AS US, BUT A WEREWOLF IS STILL A BEAST.
YOU THINK THEY'D ACCEPT THE LOVE OF A HUMAN?

THEY'RE NOT FURRY ANGELS, COURTNEY. THEY'RE WILD, LIKE FAERIES, AND DON'T ADHERE TO HUMAN STANDARDS OF GOOD AND EVIL...
...ANY MORE THAN WE DO.

COURTNEY, SUCH TRAGEDIES HAPPEN EVERY DAY. IF WE WEPT FOR THEM ALL, WE'D NEVER STOP.

LOVE DOESN'T ALWAYS CONQUER. SOMETIMES YOU HAVE TO LET IT GO AND MIND YOUR OWN BUSINESS.
COURTNEY SUDDENLY FELT AS THOUGH SHE WAS SEEING HER UNCLE FOR THE FIRST TIME.

SHE NEVER REALIZED BEFORE HOW COLD AND SHRIVELED HIS HEART MUST BE.

I HAVE GOOD NEWS, BROTHER.

THEY'RE HOLED UP IN THAT CAVE AT THE FOOT OF MOLINA HILL. WE'LL JUST WAIT FOR NIGHTFALL...

...AND PICK THEM OFF AS THEY COME OUT.
WHAT DOES IT MATTER ANYMORE?

I'LL STILL BE CURSED.

DON'T YOU SEE? IF THE BEAST IS DEAD, THE CURSE WILL LIFT. BESIDES...

DON'T YOU WANT REVENGE?

DO YOU LOVE HIM?

WHAT? PETRU? I TOLD YOU-

NO, YOU NITWIT. NOT SHOEBRUSH FACE. YOUR GYPSY FRIEND, JAN.
THEY DON'T LIKE THAT WORD. AND IT'S NONE OF YOUR-
THEY'RE GOING TO KILL HIM.

WHAT-
AND HIS PEOPLE. IF YOU DON'T HELP ME STOP THEM.

WHAT AM I SUPPOSED TO DO?
YOU'RE THE ONLY ONE THEY MIGHT LISTEN TO. BUT YOU HAVE TO OPEN YOUR MOUTH!

LEAVE ME ALONE.

YOU DON'T LOVE HIM AT ALL, DO YOU?

GOOD LUCK WITH THE MUSTACHE KING. YOU DESERVE HIM.

GOING SOMEWHERE?
SLAM

YOUNG LADY, YOU WILL GO UP TO BED THIS INSTANT, OR I'LL TURN YOU INTO A FOOTSTOOL AND SEND YOU HOME AS A SOUVENIR.

BUT-
NOT A WORD! BED!

FINE!

I KNEW YOU'D COME! I HAVE GOOD NEWS.

I THINK... I HOPE THAT BY THE MORNING, I'LL BE FREE OF THIS TERRIBLE CURSE.

WE CAN BE MARRIED AFTER ALL, MY LOVE.
WE WON'T BE MARRIED.

I DON'T WANT TO MARRY YOU, PETRU. I NEVER DID.

I DON'T LOVE YOU.

RAAAAAAAAAGH!!!

AND THE MOON ISN'T EVEN UP YET.

WHAT'S YOUR EXCUSE NOW?

THEY'RE DIFFICULT AT THAT AGE, AREN'T THEY?
AT ANY AGE.
AT LEAST YOURS DOESN'T USE WITCHCRAFT.

AS FAR AS I CAN SEE, OLD MAN, THE ONLY DIFFERENCE BETWEEN YOU AND THAT NIECE OF YOURS IS THAT YOU DON'T HAVE A KEEPER.

WE DON'T ALL NEED KEEPERS, ALEXI.
TELL THAT TO MY DAUGHTER.

MAYBE IF YOU JUST LOOSENED YOUR GRIP A LITTLE. SHE'S A GROWN WOMAN, FOR GOODNESS' SAKE.
YOU THINK I SHOULD LET HER RUN OFF WITH THAT GOD-CURSED ROMANY BOY? DON'T BE A FOOL.
I THINK PERHAPS YOU MIGHT LET HER MAKE HER OWN MISTAKES.

SOME MISTAKES CAN'T BE MENDED, ALOYSIUS. LOOK AT POOR PETRU.

I HOPE YOU'RE WRONG ABOUT THAT. OR ELSE WE'RE BOTH FOOLS.
PLEASE FORGIVE MY INTRUSION.

COURTNEY?

LISTEN, I JUST WANTED TO APOLO-

YOU OLD FOOL.

AT HOME, THE DARKNESS WAS FAMILIAR. HERE IT HAD A STRANGE TEXTURE.

SPLASH!

YOU SHOULD HAVE BROUGHT A FLASHLIGHT.

SO, DID YOU HAVE A PLAN, OR WERE YOU GOING TO STUMBLE LOST IN THE FOREST TILL DAWN?

I WAS GOING TO STAND IN FRONT OF THE CAVE AND FROWN MEANINGFULLY AT THEM.
I SEE. AND WHAT IF THEY SHOT ANYWAY? YOU'D STOP THE BULLETS?
I MIGHT.

OH, REALLY? YOU AND YOUR UNCLE MUST REALLY BE BLACK SORCERERS, LIKE PETRU SAYS.

I DON'T KNOW IF I CAN STOP THEM ALL, BUT I'LL TRY.

WHAT IF YOU CAN'T?

THEN I SUPPOSE I'LL DIE.

YOU'RE MAD.
DO YOU LOVE HIM OR NOT?

WELL?

DO YOU KNOW HOW PETRU COURTED ME? HE INVITED HIMSELF FOR DINNER AND MADE JOKES ABOUT MY COOKING. HE NEVER ACTUALLY PROPOSED, JUST HANDED OVER A RING AND SMIRKED.

JAN FOUND ME CRYING ALONE IN A CAFE. HE TOOK ME INTO THE WOODS AND PLAYED FOR ME TILL NIGHTFALL. HE MADE GOULASH WITH HIS OWN HANDS OVER A COOKING FIRE.

HE EVEN WASHED THE DISHES. I'D NEVER SEEN A MAN WASH DISHES BEFORE.

HOW CAN YOU TURN YOUR BACK ON HIM? YOU COULD BOTH, I DON'T KNOW, RUN AWAY TOGETHER, FIND SOMEPLACE NEW.

DON'T YOU SEE? I'D BE LEAVING MY WHOLE WORLD BEHIND.
SO? WHAT'S SO SPECIAL ABOUT YOUR WORLD? FROM WHAT I CAN SEE, IT'S JUST A PYRAMID OF LAZY JERKS WITH YOU AT THE BOTTOM.

ANYONE WHO'D CHOOSE **THAT** OVER **LOVE** DOESN'T KNOW WHAT LOVE **IS**.

HOW **DARE** YOU!?! YOU READ **FAIRY TALES**, AND YOU THINK YOU KNOW ALL ABOUT **LOVE**! YOU'RE JUST A **CHILD**!

YOU DON'T KNOW WHAT IT **FEELS** LIKE TO HAVE YOUR **HEART BROKEN**!

THAT'S A HELL OF A THING TO ASSUME ABOUT **ANYONE**.

PETRU? ARE YOU HUNGRY? I DON'T KNOW WHERE THAT DAUGHTER OF MINE-

...HAS GONE.

REMEMBER WHAT HAPPENED TO PETRU. DON'T BLINK, DON'T HESITATE.
STOP IT!

FOR HEAVEN'S SAKE, LOOK AT YOURSELVES! YOU'RE ACTING LIKE A BUNCH OF CHILDREN.

YOU REALLY THINK YOU'RE GOING TO FIND THE DEVIL IN THAT CAVE? WHAT IF YOU'RE WRONG? WHAT IF THERE'S ONLY A BUNCH OF FRIGHTENED ROMANY FOLK?

FELIX, WHAT IF YOU KILLED A LITTLE ROMANY CHILD? WHAT WOULD YOUR MOTHER THINK OF YOU?

THERE ARE NO WEREWOLVES! THERE'S NO EVIL HERE EXCEPT SEVEN THICK-HEADED BOYS LOOKING FOR THE DEVIL.
NO EVIL?

WHO BETRAYED MY BROTHER? WHO TEASED AND TEMPTED THAT GYPSY FIDDLE PLAYER?

LOOK ME IN THE EYE AND TELL ME YOU LOVED ONLY PETRU.
STOP IT, PAUL!

NO EVIL, GENTLEMEN? WHAT OTHER WORD FOR SUCH A WOMAN?

OKAY, I'VE HEARD ENOUGH FROM THIS GUY-

KRAK

RRAAAAAAGGhhh

PETRU!?!

THE FRUITS OF EVIL, ADULTERESS.
Raaawwr!!

WE REAP WHAT WE SOW!

BLAM

PETRU!

YOU WERE ALL JUST GOING TO STAND THERE AND LET HIM KILL MY DAUGHTER?

RRRAAAAAAAH!

GAAAH!

POP
SPOK
KRAK
KRAK
KRAK

WHAT THE HELL!?!

YOU WANT HELL, MISTER? STEP RIGHT UP.

IT'S THE CRUMRIN GIRL.
PETRU WAS RIGHT.
DEVIL CHILD.
YOUR WITCHCRAFT CAN'T HARM ME!

MAYBE NOT.

BUT THEY MIGHT.

GET AWAY, YOU ANIMALS!
LORD, PROTECT ME!

DON'T BOTHER.

SUCH PROTECTION IS FOR THE RIGHTEOUS.

NOT THE SELF-RIGHTEOUS.

PETRU THOUGHT HE HAD PROTECTION TOO.

PAPA!
IT'S NOT BAD. HE'LL BE FINE, IF THESE DEVILS WOULD LEAVE US ALONE.

DON'T WORRY, THEY WON'T-

...HURT US...

WHAT WITH THE WOUND AND HER PREVIOUS EXERTION, COURTNEY WAS TOO WOOZY TO EVEN CRY OUT.

NOT THAT THERE WAS ANY REAL NEED.

THANK YOU, FELIX.
LET'S GET YOU HOME, FATHER.
WAIT!

THE MEN CAN HELP HIM. THIS IS YOUR LAST CHANCE.

BUT...

THAT MORNING, COURTNEY FOUND THE HOUSE EMPTY BUT FOR ALOYSIUS. BY NOON, THEY'D LEFT THE VILLAGE MILES BEHIND THEM.

WAS IT **WORTH** IT?

HUH?
YOUR LITTLE ADVENTURE. THAT'S A NASTY BUMP YOU GOT. WAS IT WORTH THE RISK?

I SAVED DRAGOMIR'S PEOPLE. ISN'T THAT WORTH SOMETHING?

THIS WAS HARDLY THE FIRST TIME THEY'VE FACED SUPERSTITIOUS TOWNSPEOPLE. DRAGOMIR COULD HAVE-
FINE!

YOU'RE RIGHT. I SHOULDN'T HAVE BOTHERED!
TURNS OUT LOVE ISN'T ENOUGH AFTER ALL. IT DOESN'T MAKE MEN OUT OF ANIMALS, OR TURN COWARDS INTO HEROES, OR MAKE SPOILT LITTLE GIRLS GROW UP!

ALL THINGS CONSIDERED, LOVE IS PRETTY WORTHLESS. I DON'T SEE WHY ANYONE BOTHERS WITH IT.

Chapter Two

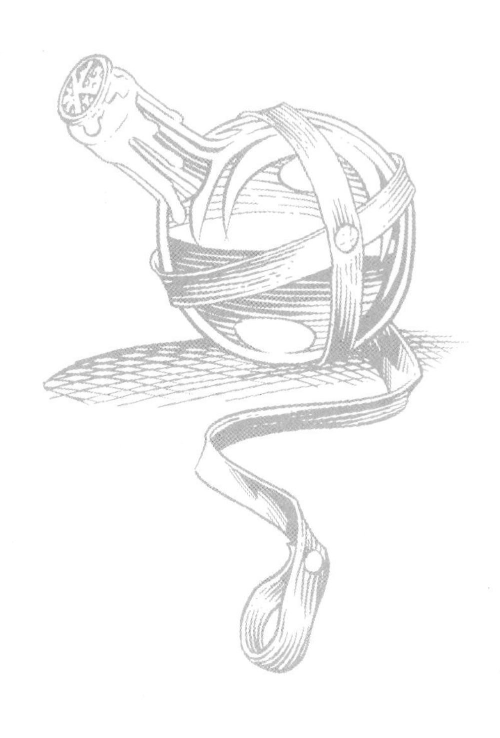

THIS FEELING HAD BEEN COURTNEY'S CONSTANT COMPANION FOR AS LONG AS SHE COULD REMEMBER.

IT CAME FLOODING BACK NOW, ALL THE WORSE BECAUSE FOR THE FIRST TIME, SHE COULD CALL IT BY NAME.

LONELINESS.

PARTS OF CASTLE KRUMRHEIN DATE BACK TO ZER ***NINTH ZENTURY***...

IT VAS VONCE ZER RULING SEAT OFF ZE HERZOGEN, ZE DUCAL FAMILY UFF KRUMRHEIN VALLEY.

HERE VE HEFF HER GRACE, ZER DUCHESS ISOLDE VON KRUMRHEIN...
WHO RULED IN ZE 15TH UNT 16TH ZENTURIES, UNT ISS PERHEPS ZE MOST VAMOUS OFF ZER HERZOGEN.

OR SHOULT I ZAY ZE MOST INVAMOUS?

ZIS VAS PAINTED JUST AFTER ZER DEATH UFF HER HUSBANT, HERZOG LEOPOLT VON KRUMRHEIN.
LADY ISOLDE, ZEN AT ZE AGE OFF TVENTY, BECOME OBZESSED MIT ZER IMMORTALITY...

...ZURROUNDING HERSELF MIT ZE ALCHEMISTS UNT DARK ZORCERERS IN A DESPERATE QVEST FOR ZER ZECRET UFF EVERLASTINK LIFE.

SHE IS KNOWN TO HEFF REIGNED FOR OVER ZEVENTY YEARSS.
TOWARD ZE ENT UFF HER REIGN, A COURTIER WROTE ZET SHE APPEARED NO DIFFERENT FROM ZIS PORTRAIT.
ZEY SAY SHE KIDNEPPED CHILDRENS FROM ZE TOWN TO DRINK THEIR BLUT.

PEASANT SUPERSTITION, NO DOUBT...
...OR VAS IT!?!
ZIS VAY PLEASE.

I TAKE IT YOU'RE NOT IMPRESSED.
HMM?
LEGEND HESS IT ZET LADY ISOLDE CONTINUED TO RULE OVER HER DESCENDANTS FROM BEYOND ZE GRAVE.

THE STORY. YOU DON'T BUY IT?
DO YOU?
DUNNO. I'VE HEARD WEIRDER.

HEARD? OR SEEN?

I'M WOLFGANG.
WOLF-?
SORRY?
NOTHING.

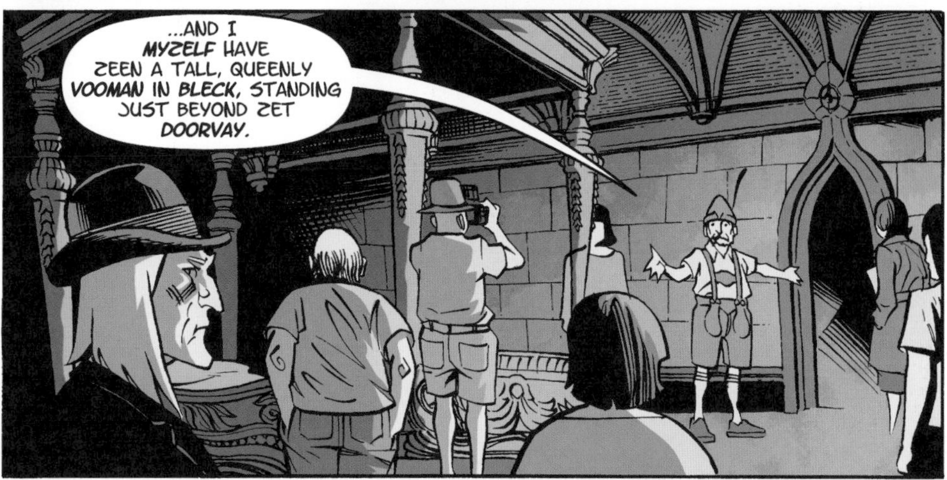
...AND I MYZELF HAVE ZEEN A TALL, QUEENLY VOOMAN IN BLECK, STANDING JUST BEYOND ZET DOORVAY.

AND VONCE AGAIN IN ZER VINDOW UFF ZER NORTH TOWER, VICH HESS BEEN INACCESSIBLE FOR ZENTURIES, EXZEPT BY HELICOPTER.

THAT ONE GOES AROUND CORNERS, RIGHT?
THE KNIGHT, YES. YOU'VE TRULY NEVER BEFORE PLAYED CHESS?

MY PARENTS PREFER GAMES WITH BRIGHTLY COLORED MONEY.

CHECKMATE.
OH, OKAY. I SHOULD MOVE MY KING AGAIN, RIGHT?

NO. THE GAME IS FINISHED.

BUT... BUT YOU HAVEN'T TAKEN MY KING. I THOUGHT THAT WAS THE POINT.
I DON'T HAVE TO. HE HAS NOWHERE TO GO, YOU SEE?

HUH...
I'M GLAD YOU'RE ENJOYING THE CASTLE...

BUT I'D RATHER YOU DIDN'T SHOW YOUR APPRECIATION BY GETTING EJECTED.

WHAT ARE YOU DOING?

>KNOCK<
>KNOCK<
>KNOCK<

YEAH?
I JUST WANTED...
I...

I WAS JUST GOING TO RETIRE. IS THERE ANYTHING YOU NEED?

I'M FINE.

VERY WELL.

IT WASN'T THAT SHE HATED HER UNCLE. SHE FELT SORRY FOR HIM.
AFTER A LIFETIME OF ISOLATION, THE MAN HAD THE EMOTIONAL EMPATHY OF A WEEVIL.

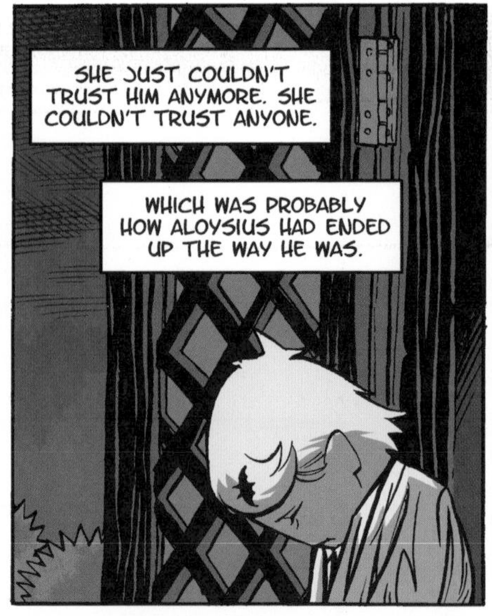
SHE JUST COULDN'T TRUST HIM ANYMORE. SHE COULDN'T TRUST ANYONE.
WHICH WAS PROBABLY HOW ALOYSIUS HAD ENDED UP THE WAY HE WAS.

OH, HELLO.

WHO'S THERE?
ONLY ME. ARE YOU ALL RIGHT?

YOU LOOK, I DON'T KNOW, WORRIED PERHAPS?

EXISTENTIAL ANGST.

WHAT IS THIS?
HECK IF I KNOW. YOU'RE THE ONE WHO SPEAKS GERMAN.

HAVE YOU EVER LOVED ANYONE?
A GIRL, YOU MEAN?
ANYONE. DO YOU LOVE YOUR PARENTS?

DOESN'T EVERYONE?

WHAT DOES IT EVEN MEAN, THOUGH? I DON'T THINK I FEEL ONE WAY OR THE OTHER ABOUT MY FOLKS. NOT REALLY.
THEY'RE JUST THESE... PEOPLE.

I KEEP HEARING ABOUT SOMETHING CALLED "UNCONDITIONAL LOVE." IT'S SUPPOSED TO FEEL LIKE THIS BIG WARM HUG ALL DAY LONG OR SOMETHING.
I NEVER FELT ANYTHING LIKE THAT. NOT ABOUT ANYBODY. PEOPLE LET YOU DOWN. THEY BREAK YOUR HEART.

THEY DIE ON YOU.

DYING IS NOT THE WORST THING.

I LOVE MY MOTHER. BUT AFTER MY FATHER DIED, SHE SEALED UP HER HEART, LITTLE BY LITTLE.
NOW SHE FEELS NOTHING.

THE HEART MUST FEEL. TO BE STRONG, IT MUST BLEED.
THEY SEAL IT TO STOP THE PAIN. THEN THE BLOOD INSIDE ROTS AND TURNS TO SLUDGE, AND THE HEART SHRIVELS UP LIKE AN OLD APPLE.
THANKS FOR THE IMAGE. WHO DO YOU MEAN?

GROWN -UPS.

MAY I COME IN?

IT'S A FREE COUNTRY.

OR IS IT?
I DIDN'T REALLY DO MUCH RESEARCH.

FINE, COME IN.

SORRY.
FOR WHAT?
I DIDN'T MEAN TO GET ALL TWEE LIKE THAT. STUPID.

DON'T DO THIS.
DON'T COVER YOUR FEELINGS. THIS IS WHAT THEY DO.

I KNOW WHERE THIS ROAD LEADS.
I AM ALONE AND I HATE IT. SOMETIMES I WANT TO SCREAM, IT HURTS SO MUCH.

BUT I FEEL NO SHAME FOR WHAT I NEED.

WHAT DO YOU NEED?

A FRIEND.

SOMEONE WHO CARES FOR ME.

LOOK, I'M SORRY. I JUST...

I...

I'M SORRY ALSO.

UNCLE A!
SOMETHING WEIRD IS GOING ON IN MY-

-ROOM...
HELLO?

COURTNEY?

WHAT ARE YOU DOING IN HERE?
ARE YOU ALL RIGHT?
I- I WAS...

I GOT SCARED. WHERE WERE YOU?

SCARED? YOU? I FIND THAT HARD TO BELIEVE.

WHAT COULD THE NIGHT HOLD THAT'S MORE FRIGHTENING THAN COURTNEY CRUMRIN?
HE HAD A POINT, OF COURSE. YET SOMEHOW, THIS WASN'T THE REACTION COURTNEY WAS HOPING FOR.
YEAH, RIGHT. SORRY TO BOTHER YOU.

OKAY, MISTER SMOOTH-TALKER GHOST GUY. I HOPE YOU KNOW WHO YOU'RE DEALING WITH.

'CAUSE WHATEVER YOU ARE NOW, MESS WITH ME AND I'LL TURN YOU INTO A PURPLE ARMADILLO.

WHAT IS THIS AWMER -DILLO?

I KNOW WHAT YOU ARE. I COULD NOT HURT YOU, EVEN IF I HAD WANTED IT.

SO WHAT'S YOUR STORY? I CAN TOUCH YOU, WHICH MEANS YOU'RE NOT A GHOST.

WHICH LEAVES...
...VAMPIRE?

ARE YOU ANGRY?

NAW. I GUESS AFTER A FEW HUNDRED YEARS, IT'S NICE TO TALK TO SOMEONE NEW.

IT WAS DISORIENTING. BEING THOUSANDS OF MILES FROM ANYTHING FAMILIAR WAS STRANGE ENOUGH.
BUT COURTNEY DIDN'T EVEN REALLY FEEL SHE HAD A HOME TO RETURN TO ANYMORE.

SHE FELT LIKE A LOST SHIP AFTER ALL THE CONTINENTS HAD SUNK UNDER THE SEA.
ZE FIRE VASS STARTED BY ZE ANGRY MOB OFF TOWN FOLK WHO BELIEVED ZE CATHEDRAL A HAVEN FOR ZE VORSHIPPERS OFF ZATAN...
...UNT BLAMED ZEM FOR ZE VANISHED CHILDREN.

...WONDERING IF THERE WERE ANY OTHER SHIPS OUT THERE ON THE ENDLESS, EMPTY OCEAN.

I THOUGHT DAYTIME WASN'T YOUR SCENE.

I AM COMPLICATED.
APPARENTLY.

THIS ONE WAS A TERRIBLE DESPOT. HE BURNED HALF THE TOWN TRYING TO ENFORCE HIS MAD TAX LAWS.

THIS ONE WAS KIND. BEING DUKE WAS ONLY EVER A BURDEN TO HIM. HE WAS MURDERED BY HIS OWN ADVISORS BEFORE HE WAS TWENTY.
WHO'S BURIED HERE?

ME.

BUT ONLY SOMETIMES.

THANK YOU FOR MEETING ME AGAIN.
WELL, I WAS THINKING OF GOING OUT CLOG DANCING WITH MY UNCLE...

...BUT YOU'RE BETTER COMPANY.

IS THIS WHAT HE TOLD YOU? THAT HE IS DANCING?
I WAS JOKING...
WAIT! YOU KNOW WHERE HE GOES AT NIGHT?

HE WENT TO THE CASTLE?

HE HAS KNOWN MY MOTHER FOR MANY YEARS.
THE DUCHESS? LADY ISOLDE?
THEY TALK FOR HOURS OF ALCHEMY AND OTHER DULL THINGS.

GEE, THANKS FOR INVITING ME...
SHE LIKES TO KEEP TRACK OF THE FAMILY, ESPECIALLY THE ONES WITH A LITTLE MAGIC.

HOLD ON... KRUMRHEIN? YOU MEAN...
HE'S, LIKE, A DESCENDANT?
THAT'S RIGHT.
SO I'M ALSO, LIKE, A VON KRUMRHEIN?

WOULD YOU LIKE TO SEE THE CASTLE AGAIN? THE NORTH TOWER, PERHAPS?
YOU GOTTA BE KIDDING...

WOW. THAT'S A HANDY TRICK.

YOU WORKED ON THE PROBLEM FOR CENTURIES. ARE YOU REALLY TELLING ME YOU HAVE NOTHING TO SHOW?

WHAT IS THIS, ALOYSIUS? YOU'VE NEVER EXPRESSED INTEREST IN THE MATTER BEFORE.
I KNOW THAT AFTER YOU CAME UPON YOUR CURRENT CONDITION, YOU CHANGED YOUR FOCUS...
IS THAT-?
SHHH.

TO A DEGREE, YES.
...SEEKING A MEANS OF RESTORING YOUR... HOW TO PHRASE IT...

MY *HUMANITY?*
I WOULDN'T HAVE PUT IT *THAT* WAY.

TIME WAS *RUNNING OUT*. MY *ELIXIRS* HAD CEASED TO BE *EFFECTIVE*.
I WAS GROWING *OLD*, ALOYSIUS. *WITHERING*. I NEEDED A *DRASTIC SOLUTION*.

YOU WERE *THIRTY-FIVE*, MADAM. HARDLY WHAT I'D CALL *DIRE STRAITS*.

YOU THINK ME *VAIN?* SHOULD I HAVE WAITED FOR THE *SECOND* WHITE HAIR? THE *THOUSANDTH?* HOW HAS THAT COURSE FARED FOR *YOU?*
TOUCHÉ.
BUT DO YOU NOT MISS YOUR *YOUTHFUL BEAUTY?*
YOU WERE NEVER SO VAIN AS *I.*

IN *ANY* EVENT, YOU THOUGHT THAT GIVEN ENOUGH *TIME,* YOU COULD FIND A CURE FOR BOTH *MORTALITY AND* VAMPIRISM.
IN THREE CENTURIES, I FOUND *NEITHER. THIS...*

...IS THE ONLY CURE FOR MORTALITY.
TAKE IT OR LEAVE IT.
I TOLD YOU BEFORE, I'LL HAVE NO PART OF...
...THAT FORM OF IMMORTALITY.

YOU SNEER, MY ARROGANT CHILD. YET YOU COME TO ME AGAIN AFTER THREE DECADES...
AS DESPERATE AS I ONCE WAS.

WHAT DRIVES YOU HITHER, IF NOT VANITY?

FOR SOME YEARS NOW, I'VE PURSUED SEVERAL LINES OF INQUIRY REGARDING A RATHER MUNDANE MALADY.

MY CRAFT CAN ONLY DELAY THE INEVITABLE, AND MY CLINIC IN SWITZERLAND HAS EXHAUSTED ITS RESEARCHES.

IT APPEARS THAT, WITHIN A YEAR, MY HEART WILL FAIL.

UNLESS I FIND A MIRACLE.

OLD FOOL. SO FULL OF SCORN ONCE, AND NOW...

DEATH IS HUMANITY'S JESTER, ALOYSIUS. HE MAKES FOOLS OF US ALL, LAUGHING AT OUR PRETENDED MAJESTY.

THIS IS THE LAST OF MY ELIXIR VITAE. I DON'T KNOW WHY I HELD ONTO IT FOR SO LONG.

TAKE IT, CHILD. IN MEMORY OF WHAT WE MIGHT HAVE BEEN TO ONE ANOTHER.

DO I WANT TO KNOW WHAT'S IN IT?
NO.

IT WILL ONLY DELAY THE INEVITABLE, ALOYSIUS.
IT WILL PULL YOU FROM THE BRINK.

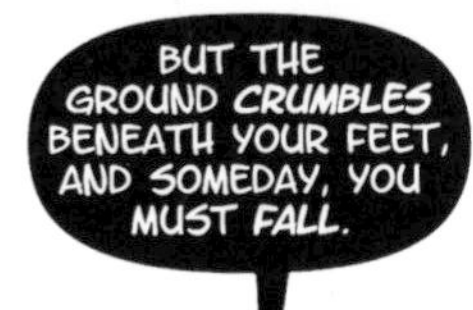
BUT THE GROUND CRUMBLES BENEATH YOUR FEET, AND SOMEDAY, YOU MUST FALL.

UNLESS, LIKE ANGELS, YOU LEARN HOW TO FLY.

COURTNEY TRIED TO SORT IT ALL OUT IN HER HEAD, BUT IT WAS USELESS. EVERY KIND OF HOPE AND FEAR SHE'D EVER KNOWN CAME CRASHING THROUGH IN A TANGLED, IMPOSSIBLE MESS.

MY FOLKS USED TO MAKE ME PLAY MONOPOLY WITH THEM. THEY WERE REALLY GOOD AT IT.
BETTER THAN I WAS, ANYWAY.

I'D START OFF WITH A LITTLE MONEY AND ALL THESE HOPES. BUT BEFORE LONG, MY MOM WOULD BUY BOARDWALK, AND I JUST KNEW I WAS DOOMED.

THING IS, THE GAME WOULD KEEP GOING AND GOING FOR HOURS.

I'M WATCHING MY MONEY DWINDLE, MY DEBTS PILE UP, MY LITTLE TRIUMPHS GETTING SOLD OFF...
...AND MY FOLKS SMIRKING.

I LIKE THIS GAME BETTER. WHEN YOU KNOW YOU CAN'T WIN, IT'S OVER.

COURTNEY! YOUR BREAKFAST IS GETTING COLD.

THIS ATTITUDE IS GETTING QUITE TIRESOME, YOUNG LADY.
>KNOCK< >KNOCK< >KNOCK<

I THINK IT'S TIME WE HAD A LITTLE-
-TALK...

IT'S A BIT OF AN EMERGENCY, I'M AFRAID.
DON'T VORRY, HERR PROFESSOR.

VE ARE A FULL SERVICE ESTABLISHMENT.

AND I'LL HAVE TO GET TO ZE MARKET BEFORE IT CLOSES. FRESH GARLIC IS MOST EFFECTIVE.
ONE OF US SHOULD WATCH HER AT ALL TIMES.

JUST VOR A CHANGE, DO YOU MEAN?

LOOK HERE, MADAM, THIS ISN'T MY FAULT. HAD COURTNEY BEEN AN ORDINARY GIRL, IT WOULD BE ONE THING. BUT SHE'S CERTAINLY MORE THAN A MATCH FOR SOME CHEEKY VAMPIRE BRAT.

SHE'S A CHILD, YOU ASS! A CHILD!
SHE'S WULNERABLE IN VAYS ZET HEFF NOTHING TO DO WISS POWER.

AND YOU'VE BEEN TREATING HER LIKE A PIECE OF INCONWENIENT BAGGAGE.

SHE DOESN'T USUALLY ACT LIKE A CHILD. SHE'S SO... MATURE.
ZMALL WONDER.

SHE PROBABLY HAD TO GROW UP FAST. AFTER ALL, WHO TAKES CARE OFF HER?

I'VE GOT TO GET TO ZE MARKET. FOR HEAVEN'S SAKE, DON'T GO VANDERING OFF AGAIN TILL I GET BECK.

I DON'T WANT TO BE RUDE, BUT DOES ANY OF THIS STUFF WORK? AND WHAT'S WITH THE CRACKERS UNDER THE WINDOW?
SACRED WAFERS, LIEBCHEN. ZER BODY OFF OUR LORD. MY PRIEST VAS KIND ENOUGH TO TRANSUBSTANTIATE ZEM IN CASE OF AN EMERGENCY.

THAT WAS NICE OF HIM. BUT DON'T THEY ONLY WORK IF I BELIEVE IN THEM OR SOMETHING?
DON'T YOU?
IN CRACKERS? NOT REALLY.

ALOYSIUS SAID THAT CHRISTIAN MAGIC CAN WORK, BUT ONLY IF YOU BUY INTO THE WHOLE SON OF GOD THING, AT LEAST A LITTLE BIT. WHICH I DON'T.
SORRY. NO OFFENSE.

NONE TAKEN. IT DOESN'T METTER VAT YOU BELIEF. IT'S VAT YOUR LITTLE FRIEND BELIEVES ZET COUNTS.
YOU MEAN WOLFGANG? NOW YOU REALLY LOST ME.

YOUR UNCLE HESS TAUGHT YOU ZE OLD MAGIC, FROM BEFORE ZE WORD OFF ZE LORD CAME TO EUROPE.
BUT ZE LORD'S POWER ISN'T SO DIFFERENT. IT HESS ITS DARK SIDE TOO, LIKE YOURS.
IT DOES?

HIS POWER IS IN GOODNESS. BUT BENT BECKWARD, EVIL FOR ITS OWN SAKE HESS ITS REWARDS. YOU SEE?
NOT REALLY.

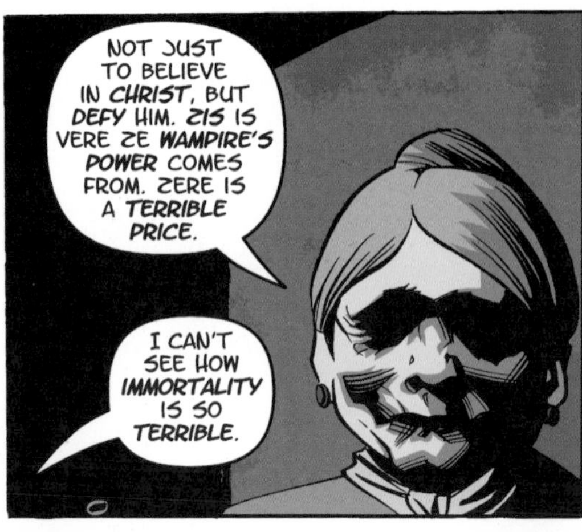
NOT JUST TO BELIEVE IN CHRIST, BUT DEFY HIM. ZIS IS VERE ZE WAMPIRE'S POWER COMES FROM. ZERE IS A TERRIBLE PRICE.
I CAN'T SEE HOW IMMORTALITY IS SO TERRIBLE.

I VASN'T ALWAYS AN OLD WOMAN, YOU KNOW. HE CAME TO ME VEN I VAS YOUR AGE.
HE PROMISED IMMORTAL LIFE, EVERLASTING LOVE. I KNEW BETTER.

I VONCE SAW AN AMERICAN MOVIE VERE A FAT LITTLE GHOST GORGED HIMSELF ON CORPOREAL FOOD. AS HE SVALLOWED, IT FELL TO ZE FLOOR.
ZET IS YOUR VOLFGANG.

HE ZINKS HE'S OFFERING ETERNAL LIFE. BUT HE HESS NO TRUE LIFE TO GIVE.

HE HUNGERS FOR LOVE.
BUT LOVE CANNOT NURTURE THE DEAD.

COURTNEY WASN'T SURE IF SHE WAS SEEING THINGS IN THIS WORLD ANYMORE.

WAS SHE STARING INTO HELL?

OR WAS THIS WHAT THE WORLD REALLY LOOKED LIKE?

IT DIDN'T SEEM TO MATTER.

THE GAME WAS OVER.

ARE YOU READY TO *GO*?

FORGETTING SOMETHING?

YOU'RE SUPPOSED TO SUCK UP TO HER OLD MAN.

RAAAAAAWWWW

THUNK
ARRRRGH!

GAAH!

GET DOWN!

GRRROOOOWWLLL

STALE TRICKS, BOY. HAVEN'T YOU LEARNED ANYTHING NEW OVER THE CENTURIES?
RAAAAAACCCHHHH!

UNCLE A?

AND THIS TRICK? TOO OLD FOR YOU?
DON'T HURT HIM!

CAN YOU FLY, MORTAL?

OF COURSE I CAN FLY, YOU NINCOMPOOP. I'M A WARLOCK.

...

BOOOMMM

YOUR CONCERN WAS TOUCHING, I MUST SAY. THOUGH I FEAR YOUR PLEAS FELL ON DEAF EARS.

NO KIDDING. I WASN'T TALKING TO HIM.
IT ISN'T OVER. HE VON'T STOP NOW.

WE CAN BE GONE BY NIGHTFALL TOMORROW.
SHE'S IN NO SHAPE TO TRAVEL. BESIDES, IT VON'T METTER. HER BLOOD CALLS TO HIM.

HE'LL FOLLOW HER ACROSS ZE VORLD. UNLESS HE'S DESTROYED.
OR SHE FORSAKES HIM UTTERLY.

COURTNEY, YOU SAW WHAT HE IS. YOU DON'T WANT ANYTHING TO DO WITH HIM, DO YOU?

JUST CLOSE YOUR HEART TO HIM, AND IT'LL BE OVER.

GO TO HELL.

I REPLACED THE CROSSES AND NAILED UP THE DOORS. THEY SHOULD HOLD.
NOT IF SHE WANTS OUT.

I'M GOING FOR A WALK. KEEP AN EYE ON HER TILL I GET BACK.

YOU SHOULD BE IN BED.

I'M NOT HUNGRY.
YOU VILL BE LATER. VONE VAY OR ZE OTHER.

YOU SAW ZE CHILDREN, DIDN'T YOU?
YES.
THEN YOU KNOW WHAT YOU MUST BECOME.

SURELY YOUR LIFE ISN'T SO BAD THAT ETERNAL HOPELESSNESS SEEMS BETTER.
I'M SICK OF HOPE. I KNOW WHERE IT LEADS.
YEAR AFTER YEAR, HOPING THAT SOMEONE WILL COME ALONG WHO DOESN'T LET ME DOWN.

UNTIL I'M GOD KNOWS HOW OLD AND TRYING TO HOLD OFF DEATH JUST A LITTLE LONGER. FOR WHAT?
LOSING SHOULDN'T TAKE THAT LONG.

WHAT ARE YOU DOING HERE?

I SHOULD THINK IT OBVIOUS.

>SNORT<

VERDAMMT!

YOU THINK YOU CAN DEFEAT ME, MORTAL?

I CAN BECOME WOLF, BIRD OF PREY, VAPOR. YOUR FIRE, YOUR SWORD, YOUR WOODEN STAKES...

THESE THINGS CANNOT HARM VAPOR.
I DON'T INTEND TO FIGHT YOU.

I'M JUST WAITING TO SEE WHICH GRAVE YOU RETURN TO.

OTHERWISE I'D BE ALL DAY SEARCHING.

I'M FAMILIAR WITH YOUR POWERS. ALL OF THEM.

MOST ARE JUST SORCERER'S TRICKS YOUR MOTHER TAUGHT YOU.

TOO BAD YOU'RE SUCH A POOR STUDENT.
STOP IT!

LEAVE HIM ALONE, PLEASE! CAN'T YOU SEE HE'S ALREADY HURT!?!

COURTNEY! YOU SHOULDN'T BE HERE!

SO YOU CAN PLAY YOUR LITTLE GAMES IN SECRET? LIKE IN ROMANIA?
I ONLY MEANT TO KEEP YOU OUT OF DANGER. I DIDN'T WANT YOU TO SEE THIS.
SEE WHAT? THAT YOU'RE A BULLY?

LOOK, YOU'VE WON. YOU DON'T HAVE TO MAKE IT WORSE.

I'M USED TO THIS CRAP FROM MY PARENTS.
BUT ALL THESE STUPID GAMES...

YOU WERE SUPPOSED TO KNOW BETTER.

YOU'RE RIGHT. I'M SORRY.

I'VE NEVER BEEN GOOD AT TAKING CARE OF ANYONE.
OBVIOUSLY.
I DON'T NEED TAKEN CARE OF. I JUST...
I DON'T KNOW.

I QUITE UNDERSTAND.

I GRANTED YOU AUDIENCE. I GAVE YOU GIFTS.
I OFFERED ETERNAL LIFE!
UH-OH.

THIS IS HOW YOU REPAY ME!?!

GET HOME, COURTNEY! RUN!
BUT-

HOW DARE YOU!?!
GO!

MY POWERS MAY BE ONLY SORCERY AS YOU SAY...

BUT I'VE HAD CENTURIES TO HONE THEM.
VERY WELL.

LET US SEE WHO'S THE BETTER SORCERER.

YOU TRICKY...

RUN, COURTNEY.

COURTNEY, PLEASE! I NEED YOU.

SO HUNGRY...

IS THIS WHAT YOU WANTED, ALOYSIUS?
IS THIS BETTER THAN LIFE EVERLASTING?

MAYBE NOT.

BUT THE VIEW IS BETTER.

FOOOMMMFF

WE'LL BE TOGETHER *FOREVER*.
WE'LL *NEVER* BE LONELY *AGAIN*.

I BET YOU SAY THAT TO ALL THE GIRLS.

SORRY, UNCLE A. IT'S TOO LATE.
THREE BITES.

GAME OVER.
CHECKMATE.

IT'S NOT LIKE YOU TO GIVE UP SO EASILY.

THE TRICK IS TO CHANGE THE RULES.
WHAT GAME YOU'RE PLAYING IS UP TO YOU.

HERE.

YOU MIGHT FIND THIS USEFUL.
©1936
Chance
GET OUT OF JAIL FREE

WHAT'S THAT NOISE?

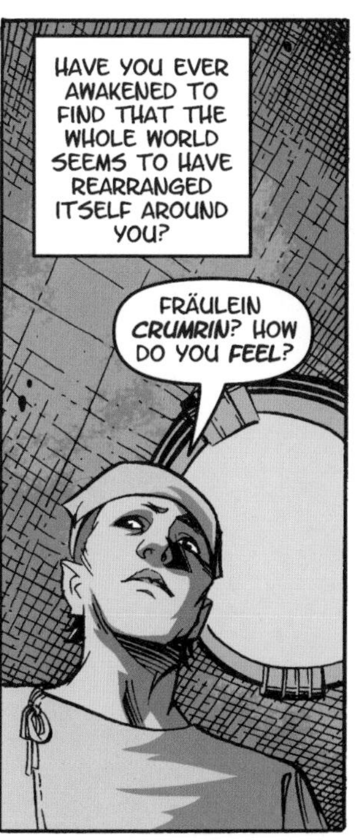
HAVE YOU EVER AWAKENED TO FIND THAT THE WHOLE WORLD SEEMS TO HAVE REARRANGED ITSELF AROUND YOU?
FRÄULEIN CRUMRIN? HOW DO YOU FEEL?

YOU JUST HAVE TO PICK UP THE STORY AS BEST YOU CAN.
LIKE BEEF JERKY. WHO'RE YOU?
I'M HANS. I'M A NURSE HERE.
HERE?
YOU'RE IN SWITZERLAND.

THIS IS THE CLINIQUE LA PRAIRIE.
IT'S AMAZING YOU'RE ALIVE AFTER LOSING MOST OF YOUR BLOOD SUPPLY.

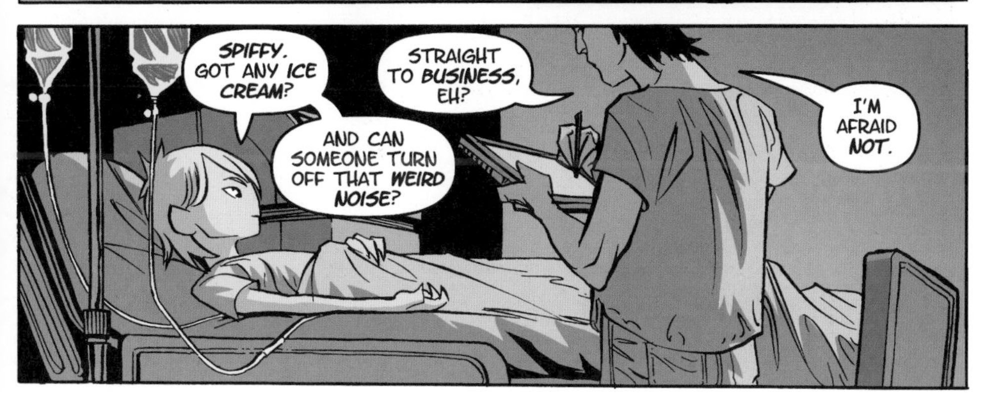
SPIFFY. GOT ANY ICE CREAM?
AND CAN SOMEONE TURN OFF THAT WEIRD NOISE?
STRAIGHT TO BUSINESS, EH?
I'M AFRAID NOT.

YOUR UNCLE INSISTED YOU STAY WHERE HE COULD KEEP AN EYE ON YOU.
ZZZZZZZZZ...

UNFORTUNATELY, HE SNORES LIKE A STEAM ENGINE.
ZZZZZZZZZZZZZZ...

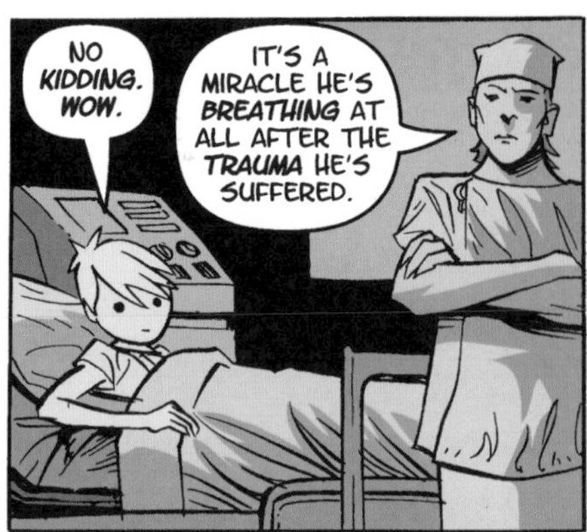
NO KIDDING. WOW.
IT'S A MIRACLE HE'S BREATHING AT ALL AFTER THE TRAUMA HE'S SUFFERED.

AND AT HIS AGE, TOO. MUST BE TOUGH AS NAILS.
HE ALWAYS SEEMS TO HAVE AN EXTRA "GET OUT OF JAIL FREE" CARD HANDY.

Courtney Crumrin

By Ted Naifeh

Monstrous Holiday

Bonus Material & Cover Gallery

Cover artwork for the *The Fire Thief's Tale*.

Cover artwork for the *The Prince of Nowhere*.

Cover artwork for the original softcover collection of *Monstrous Holiday*.

A promo image created for the *Courtney Crumrin* art exhibit at the Galerie Arludik.

Pencil concept sketches to work out Courtney's European look.

Pencil sketches to work out the look of the wolves.

Early pencil sketches for the *Prince of Nowhere*.

Ted Naifeh

Ted Naifeh first appeared in the independent comics scene in 1999 as the artist for *Gloomcookie*, the goth romance comic he co-created with Serena Valentino for SLG Publishing. After a successful run, Ted decided to strike out on his own, writing and drawing *Courtney Crumrin and the Night Things*, a spooky children's fantasy series about a grumpy little girl and her adventures with her Warlock uncle.

Nominated for an Eisner Award for best limited series, *Courtney Crumrin*'s success paved the way for *Polly and the Pirates*, another children's book, this time about a prim and proper girl kidnapped by pirates convinced she was the daughter of their long-lost queen.

Over the next few years, Ted wrote four volumes of *Courtney Crumrin*, plus a spin-off book about her uncle. He also co-created *How Loathsome* with Tristan Crane, and illustrated two volumes of the videogame tie-in comic *Death Junior* with screenwriter Gary Whitta. More recently, he illustrated *The Good Neighbors*, a three volume graphic novel series written by *New York Times* bestselling author Holly Black, published by Scholastic.

In 2011, Ted wrote the sequel to *Polly and the Pirates*, and illustrated several *Batman* short stories for DC Comics. In 2012, to celebrate the 10th anniversary of *Courtney Crumrin*, he wrote and illustrated the final two volumes of the series. Currently, you can find Ted everywhere: from the pages of *Batman '66* to his newest original series for adults, *Night's Dominion*.

Ted lives in San Francisco, because he likes dreary weather.

Courtney Crumrin

By Ted Naifeh

Keep Reading Courtney Crumrin:

Courtney Crumrin, Volume 1:
The Night Things
By Ted Naifeh
136 pages • 6"x9" Softcover • Color
ISBN 978-1-62010-419-4

Courtney Crumrin, Volume 2:
The Coven of Mystics
By Ted Naifeh
144 pages • 6"x9" Softcover • Color
ISBN 978-1-62010-463-7

Courtney Crumrin, Volume 3:
The Twilight Kingdom
by Ted Naifeh and Warren Wucinich
144 pages • 6"x9" Softcover • Color
ISBN: 978-1-62010-518-4

Courtney Crumrin, Volume 5:
The Witch Next Door
by Ted Naifeh
144 pages • 6"x9" Hardcover • Color
ISBN: 978-1-934964-96-5

Courtney Crumrin, Volume 6:
The Final Spell
By Ted Naifeh
152 pages • 6"x9" Hardcover • Color
ISBN: 978-1-62010-018-9

Courtney Crumrin, Volume 7:
Tales of a Warlock
by Ted Naifeh
128 pages • 6"x9" Hardcover • Color
ISBN: 978-1-62010-019-6

More by Ted Naifeh

Polly And The Pirates
By Ted Naifeh
176 pages • Digest • Black & White
ISBN 978-1-932664-46-1

Princess Ugg, Volume 1
By Ted Naifeh
120 pages • Softcover • Color
ISBN 978-1-62010-178-0

Princess Ugg, Volume 2
By Ted Naifeh
120 pages • Softcover • Color
ISBN 978-1-62010-215-2

For more information on these and other fine Oni Press comic books and graphic novels, visit www.onipress.com. To find a comic specialty store in your area, call 1-888-COMICBOOK or visit, www.comicshops.us.